Other books by Mick Inkpen

ONE BEAR AT BEDTIME
THE BLUE BALLOON
THREADBEAR

This book is a presentation of Newfield Publications, Inc.
Newfield Publications offers book clubs for children
from preschool through high school. For further
information write to: **Newfield Publications, Inc.,**
4343 Equity Drive, Columbus, Ohio 43228.

Reprinted by arrangement with Little, Brown and Company, (Inc.).
Newfield Publications is a trademark
of Newfield Publications, Inc.
Weekly Reader is a federally registered trademark
of Weekly Reader Corporation.
Printed in the United States of America.

First U.S. Edition 1992

Library of Congress Cataloging-in-Publication Data

Inkpen, Mick.
Kipper/Mick Inkpen. – 1st U.S. ed.

p.    cm.

Summary: Tired of his old blanket and basket, Kipper the dog
searches among the animals outside for a new place to sleep.
ISBN 0-316-41883-8
[1. Dogs – Fiction.    2. Animals – Fiction.]    I. Title.
PZ7.1564Ki    1992
[E] – dc20                                    90-53693

First published in Great Britain in 1991
by Hodder and Stoughton Children's Books

10  9  8  7  6  5  4  3  2  1

*Weekly Reader Children's Book Club Presents*

# Kipper

## Mick Inkpen

### Little, Brown and Company
Boston   Toronto   London

Kipper was in the mood for tidying
his basket.

'You are falling apart!' he said
to his rabbit.

'You are chewed and you are soggy!'
he said to his ball and his bone.

'And you are DISGUSTING!' he said
to his smelly old blanket.

Out they went.
'That's better!' said Kipper.

But it was not better. Now his basket was uncomfortable.

He twisted and he turned. He wiggled and he wriggled. But it was no good. He could not get comfortable.

'Silly basket!' said Kipper…

…and went outside.

Outside there were two ducks.
They looked very comfortable
standing on one leg.

'That's what I should do!' said
Kipper. But he wasn't very good.
He could only…

...wobble.

Some wrens had made a nest inside
a flowerpot. It looked very cosy.
    'I should sleep in one of those!'
said Kipper. But Kipper would not fit
inside a flowerpot.

He was much too big!

The squirrels had made their nest
out of sticks.

'I will build myself a stick nest!'
said Kipper. But Kipper's nest was
not very good. He could only find…

...three sticks!

The sheep looked very happy
just sitting in the grass.
No, that was no good either.
The grass was much too...

...tickly!

The frog had found a sunny place
in the middle of the pond.
He was sitting on a lily pad.
   'I wonder if I could do that,'
said Kipper.

But he couldn't!

'Perhaps a nice dark hole
would be good,' thought Kipper.
'The rabbits seem to like them.'

But it was not
a rabbit hole!

Kipper rushed indoors and hid underneath his blanket.

His

lovely

old

smelly

blanket!

Kipper put the blanket back in his basket. He found his rabbit.

'Sorry Rabbit,' he said.

He found his bone and his ball.

'I like my basket just the way it is,' yawned Kipper. He climbed in and pulled the blanket over his head.

'It is the best basket in the whole, wide...

...sssssssssssh

hhhhhh!